CHRISTOPHER BEAR'S FIRST CHRISTMAS

STEPHANIE JEFFS

ILLUSTRATED BY FRANK ENDERSBY

Everywhere Joe went,
Christopher Bear went too.
One day Joe went to pre-school.
There were twinkling lights
on the playhouse.
And the hobby horse was
eating hay from a bag.
'It's because it's nearly Christmas,'
Miss Rosie said.

Joe and Harry sat at the table with scissors and glue.
'Today we're making shiny stars,' said Miss Rosie.
Harry and Joe worked very hard.
Christopher Bear did too.
'Look at my star!' said Harry.

It was big and covered in glitter.
Christopher Bear just smiled
his crooked smile
made of button-thread.

7

Joe went to play with the farm.
Elizabeth was counting the sheep.
'Look at the baby lambs!' she said.

And she gave one to Christopher Bear to hold.
'I've got a new baby brother,' said Elizabeth.
'But I'm not allowed to hold him yet.'

9

'Come over here, Joe!' called Miss Rosie.
And she gave him some shiny wings
from the dressing-up box.

10

Joe and Christopher Bear
danced together.
'We're flying!' said Joe.

11

'We're going to have our story soon,' said Miss Rosie.
'But first of all, I need some help.'

She rummaged in the dressing-up box.
'You can be Mary,' she said,
giving Elizabeth a blue cloak.
'And you can be Joseph,'
she said to Ben.
She put a tea towel on his head.

'Here's your donkey.'
Miss Rosie gave Ben the
hobby horse.

14

'Joe and Elizabeth can help me fill the cot with straw.'
They carried the cot to the story mat.
Christopher Bear went along for the ride.

All the children sat on the story mat.
'This is the story of the very first Christmas,'
began Miss Rosie.
'Long ago, on the very first Christmas night,
a bright star twinkled in the sky.'
Harry held up his star for everyone to see.

'On the first Christmas night,' said Miss Rosie, 'there were shepherds looking after their sheep outside a town called Bethlehem.'
Jessie, Oliver and Amelie held up the sheep and lambs.

19

'Angels sang in the sky that night,' said Miss Rosie, 'because something very special had happened.'

20

Joe stood up, and showed everyone his wings.
'On the very first Christmas,' said Miss Rosie,
'God sent his Son to be born as a baby.'

Miss Rosie held out her hand to Ben and Elizabeth.

Mary was going to have a baby,'
said Miss Rosie.
'But there was no room for them
to stay at the inn.'

'Mary and Joseph had
travelled a long way,
but at last they came
to Bethlehem.

23

'That night Mary had her baby in a stable, and she made him a bed in the manger.' Just then, Elizabeth's mummy came into pre-school. She was carrying Elizabeth's new baby brother. She put the baby gently into the cot full of hay.

'Who was the baby in the manger?' whispered Joe. 'It was Jesus,' replied Miss Rosie, 'God's Son.'

All the children looked at the baby.
Everyone was quiet, thinking about the baby Jesus,
God's Son, sleeping in a manger.

28

Joe squeezed Christopher Bear.
And Christopher Bear just smiled his crooked smile
made of button-thread.

PALM TREE

Buxhall, Stowmarket, Suffolk IP14 3BW
Tel: +44 (0) 1449 737978 E-mail: info@kevinmayhew.com
www.kevinmayhew.com

Product Code: 1600012   ISBN: 978 1 83858 015 5

First edition 2002
This UK edition 2019

Publishing Director: Annette Reynolds
Art Director: Gerald Rogers
Pre-production: Doug Hewitt

Printed and bound in Malaysia